Dear Parent:

Congratulations! Your child is taking the first steps on an exciting journey. The destination? Independent reading!

STEP INTO READING® will help your child get there. The program offers five steps to reading success. Each step includes fun stories and colorful art. There are also Step into Reading Sticker Books, Step into Reading Math Readers, Step into Reading Phonics Readers, Step into Reading Write-In Readers, and Step into Reading Phonics Boxed Sets—a complete literacy program with something for every child.

Learning to Read, Step by Step!

Ready to Read   Preschool–Kindergarten
• big type and easy words • rhyme and rhythm • picture clues
For children who know the alphabet and are eager to begin reading.

Reading with Help   Preschool–Grade 1
• basic vocabulary • short sentences • simple stories
For children who recognize familiar words and sound out new words with help.

Reading on Your Own   Grades 1–3
• engaging characters • easy-to-follow plots • popular topics
For children who are ready to read on their own.

Reading Paragraphs   Grades 2–3
• challenging vocabulary • short paragraphs • exciting stories
For newly independent readers who read simple sentences with confidence.

Ready for Chapters   Grades 2–4
• chapters • longer paragraphs • full-color art
For children who want to take the plunge into chapter books but still like colorful pictures.

STEP INTO READING® is designed to give every child a successful reading experience. The grade levels are only guides. Children can progress through the steps at their own speed, developing confidence in their reading, no matter what their grade.

Remember, a lifetime love of reading starts with a single step!

Barbie i can be...

Story Collection

Visit us on the Web!
StepIntoReading.com
randomhouse.com/kids
www.barbie.com

Educators and librarians, for a variety of teaching tools, visit us at
RHTeachersLibrarians.com

ISBN 978-0-449-81666-0

MANUFACTURED IN CHINA
10 9 8 7 6 5 4 3 2 1

Random House Children's Books supports the First Amendment and celebrates the right to read.

i can be...
Barbie™
Story Collection

A Horse Rider

A Pet Vet

A Baby Doctor

A Teacher

A Ballerina

Step 1 and Step 2 Books

A Collection of Five Early Readers

Random House 🏠 New York

Contents

I Can Be a Horse Rider 9

I Can Be a Pet Vet 39

I Can Be a Baby Doctor 69

I Can Be a Teacher 99

I Can Be a Ballerina 129

STEP INTO READING®

STEP 1

A Horse Rider

Concept developed for Mattel by Egmont Creative Center

Adapted by Mary Man-Kong

Illustrated by JiYoung An and TJ Team

Random House 🏠 New York

Barbie and her sister
Chelsea love horses.

Barbie rides

on the side.

Barbie twirls a rope.

She ropes a cow.

Barbie rides

around a barrel.

Barbie loves
her horse, Tawny.

Barbie takes Chelsea to the stable.

Barbie teaches Chelsea.

They saddle Starlight.

Chelsea's class goes
on a trail ride.

Barbie teaches Tawny.

They trot!

They jump!

Tawny will not jump
over the log fence.

Barbie tells Tawny
it will be okay.

Tawny will still
not jump.

Barbie and her friends

get small logs.

Barbie makes
a small log fence.

Barbie keeps
Tawny calm.

Tawny jumps
over the log fence!

Where is Chelsea?

Barbie must find
her sister!

Barbie finds a clue.

It is Chelsea's ribbon.

A big log is
in Barbie's way.

Tawny jumps
over the log!

Barbie finds Chelsea!

She is safe.

Chelsea is proud
of Barbie.

Barbie is proud
of Tawny.

Barbie is a good
horse rider!

Barbie™ i can be...

A Pet Vet

By Mary Man-Kong

Illustrated by Jiyoung An

Random House 🏠 New York

Barbie takes her pet to the vet.

A vet helps pets.

The vet checks Lacey.

Lacey is okay.

The busy vet
needs help.

Barbie will help the vet.

What pets will they help?

Big dog.

Small kittens.

Gray cat.

49

Blue bird.

Fluffy bunny.

Bumpy turtle.

Barbie and the vet
help all the pets.

Barbie brings Ken's dog
to the scale.

Lacey helps.

The kittens are next.
Where did they go?

Teresa looks up.

Barbie looks down.
They find
the kittens!

Barbie pats Nikki's sick cat.

The vet helps
the cat.

What pet is next?

A pony!

The pony hurt
its leg.

The vet checks it.

Barbie and the vet
help the pony.

Barbie can be

a pet vet, too.

Hooray for vets!

Hooray for pets!

STEP INTO READING®

STEP 2

Barbie I can be...
A Baby Doctor

Concept developed for Mattel by Egmont Creative Center

By Susan Marenco based on plots written by Giulia Conti

Adapted by Kristen L. Depken

Illustrated by Tino Santanach and Joaquin Canizares
with Pam Duarte

Random House 🏠 New York

Barbie wants
to be a baby doctor.
She goes
to the hospital.

She visits babies
in the nursery.
She will learn
to take care of them!

Barbie meets
Doctor Green.
She is a baby doctor.

Barbie meets
Nurse Kay.
She is a baby nurse.
They will teach Barbie
to take care of babies.

Barbie holds

a baby boy.

He starts to cry!

Barbie rocks

the baby.

He cries and cries.

Nurse Kay says
the baby is hungry.
She gets a bottle.

Barbie feeds the baby.

He stops crying!

The baby is done eating.
Nurse Kay shows Barbie
how to burp him.

Barbie puts the baby
on her shoulder.
She pats his back.
He burps!

Barbie smells
something funny.
The baby has
a dirty diaper.

Barbie changes the baby's diaper.

Later she
gives him a bath.

It is time to play!

Barbie puts

the babies

on a mat.

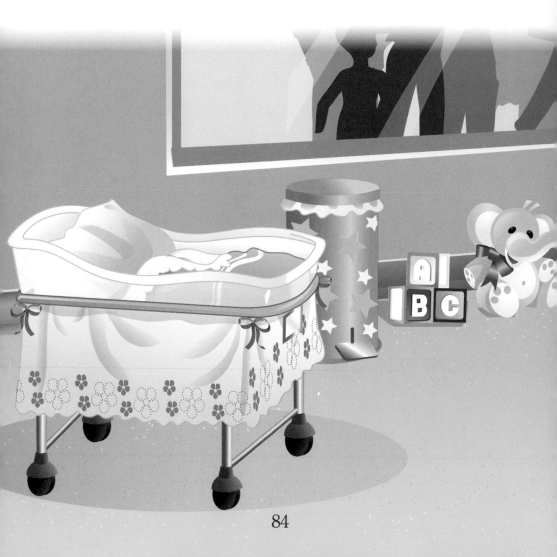

She shows them

a toy.

The babies love it!

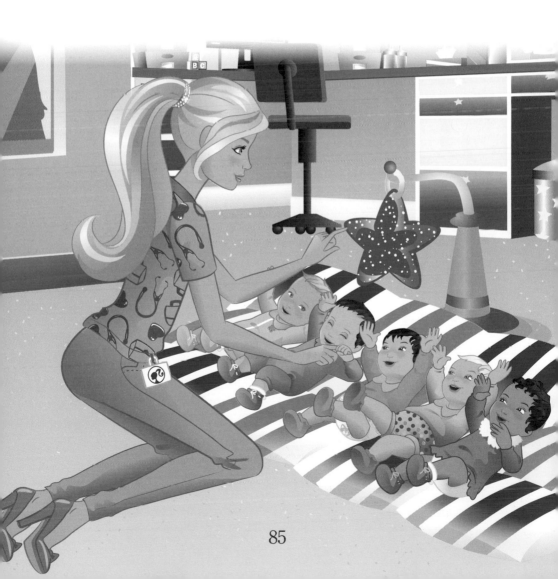

It is nap time!
Barbie and Doctor Green
put the babies
in their cribs.

They wrap the babies
in blankets.

Soon all the babies
are asleep.

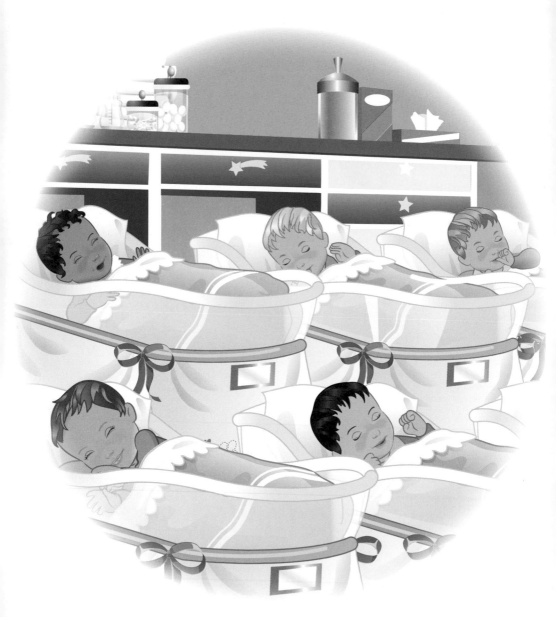

Another doctor comes
to the nursery.
He asks Barbie
and Nurse Kay
for help.

Barbie and Nurse Kay meet a new baby girl.

They will take care
of the baby
while her mom rests.

Nurse Kay shows Barbie
how to hold
the new baby.
She is so tiny!

Barbie gives the baby
her first bath.

Barbie dresses the baby.

Then Barbie
brings the baby
to her mom.
The mom
will feed the baby.

Barbie shows the mom
how to burp the baby.
Doctor Green checks
on them.
Barbie does a great job!

The baby's
mom and dad
thank Barbie.

One day,

Barbie will be

a great baby doctor!

Barbie i can be...
A Teacher

By Mary Man-Kong
Illustrated by Kellee Riley

Random House 🏠 New York

Miss Jones is a teacher.

Barbie learns to be a teacher, too.

She helps teach a class.

The class is happy
to see Barbie.
They show her
their schoolwork.

Anna shows Barbie
around the classroom.

Anna shows Barbie
the class pets.

Barbie helps feed
the cute bunnies
and the furry hamster.

Maggie gives the bunny
a carrot.
Maggie loves pets.

One day,
she can be
a pet vet.

Miss Jones makes
a reading circle.

She reads a book
to the class.

The class writes
their own stories.
Barbie helps.

Emily writes

a princess story.

Emily loves
to write.
One day, she can
be an author.

The kids study
sea animals.

Barbie makes animal art
with them.

Suzy paints a crab.

Suzy loves
sea animals.
One day, she can be
a marine biologist.

It is snack time!

Barbie helps

the class.

They make cupcakes!

Kate loves to bake.

One day,

she can be a chef.

Barbie teaches the
kids about space.

She shows the class
pictures of stars
and planets.

Lisa finds pictures

of the planets.

Lisa loves space.
One day, she can be
an astronaut.

Anna likes
to help Barbie.

She likes
to help Miss Jones.
And she likes
to help other kids.

Anna has an idea.
One day, she can be
a teacher!

Barbie thinks Anna
will be a great
teacher.
Barbie can be
a teacher, too!

Barbie i can be...

A Ballerina

By Christy Webster

Illustrated by Kellee Riley

Random House 🏠 New York

Barbie loves to dance.
Today she has
ballet class.

Barbie and Teresa take ballet together.

The girls practice
the positions.

First, second, third, fourth, and fifth.

Barbie leaps

across the room.

Teresa stands
on her toes.

Barbie and Teresa
want to be ballerinas
in a ballet company.

A ballet company
is a group
of ballet dancers.
Dancing is their job!

The teacher invites
Barbie and Teresa
to meet a real ballerina.

The next day,
Barbie and Teresa
visit the City Ballet.

They meet Becca.
She is a ballerina
in the City Ballet.

Barbie and Teresa
spend the day
with her.

They go
to the dressing room.
Becca shows them
her locker.

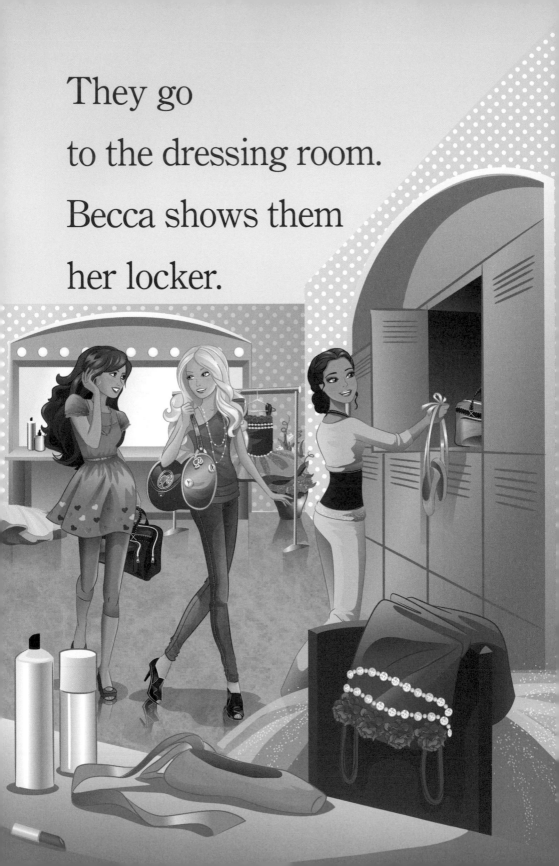

The girls put on
their ballet shoes.

Becca takes
Barbie and Teresa
to ballet class.

They meet
the other dancers.
Barbie and Teresa
join the class.

First,

they stretch.

The dancers stand

at the barre.

They point their toes
to the front, side,
and back.

They move their arms
up and down.

The dancers
take turns leaping.
The teacher watches.
The class is like
Barbie and Teresa's
class.

After lunch,
the dancers practice
for their show.
They practice
on the stage.

They dance
the same steps
over and over.

Becca is the star!
She practices her solo.

The director needs
two more dancers.

Barbie and Teresa
will play small parts
in the ballet!

Becca teaches
Barbie and Teresa
the steps.

Then they put
on their costumes.

It is time for
the show!
Barbie and Teresa
can be ballerinas!